In the Buff

In the Buff

Vicki Grant

ORCA BOOK PUBLISHERS

Library and Archives Canada Cataloguing in Publication

Grant, Vicki, author
In the buff / Vicki Grant.
(Orca currents)

Issued in print and electronic formats.
ISBN 978-1-4598-1882-8 (softcover).—ISBN 978-1-4598-1883-5 (PDF).—
ISBN 978-1-4598-1884-2 (EPUB)

I. Title. II. Series: Orca currents
PS8613.R36715 2018   jC813'.6   C2017-907700-7
                            C2017-907701-5

First published in the United States, 2018
Library of Congress Control Number: 2018933743

Summary: In this high-interest novel for middle readers,
Rupert visits his grandfather, Gump, at a nudist colony, and the two
of them get lost in the woods while searching for Gump's beloved dog.
A free teacher guide for this title is available at orcabook.com.

*Orca Book Publishers is dedicated to preserving the environment and has
printed this book on Forest Stewardship Council® certified paper.*

Orca Book Publishers gratefully acknowledges the support for its
publishing programs provided by the following agencies: the Government
of Canada through the Canada Book Fund and the Canada Council for the
Arts, and the Province of British Columbia through the BC Arts
Council and the Book Publishing Tax Credit.

Edited By Tanya Trafford
Cover photography by iStock.com/PeopleImages
Author photo by Megan Tansey Whitton

ORCA BOOK PUBLISHERS
orcabook.com

Printed and bound in Canada.

21 20 19 18 • 4 3 2 1

For my younger brother,
D.A. Grant, AB, LLB, MD
and most of all, FLK.
In memory of his many attempts to
flee naked from our clutches.

Chapter One

My grandfather's name is Alan J. Smithers, but everyone calls him Gump. He's old and he's skinny and he's really cranky.

He's also naked.

Like, totally butt naked.

And not just at bath time. I'm talking 24/7.

I'm used to the old, skinny, cranky part of him. I'm even kind of okay with it. He's been like that for as long as I can remember. The butt-naked part is new, though, and I don't like it.

I don't even get it. Gump used to be quite a "snappy dresser," at least in his humble opinion. His clothes were always super colorful and tucked in nice and tight. He was a big fan of matching socks and golf shirts, usually striped. I guess if you're seventy-five that's pretty snazzy, but to me he just looked kind of like the world's oldest preschooler, all ready for picture day.

Not that I cared. If it made him happy, fine by me. In fact, if it made him even slightly less *un*happy, that worked too.

When I was little, I used to have a lot of fun with Gump. Back then we spent all our time together. We mostly did old-guy stuff like fishing or bowling or screaming at the TV during the hockey playoffs, but I liked it. Gump is old, but he was never boring. He liked to break rules. We always went fishing at the pond with the No Fishing sign or tried to see how hard we could lob the balls at the bowling alley. He'd get pretty mouthy if we ever got caught, but nobody seemed to mind. When you're that age, people let you get away with stuff. They even think it's cute.

Well, it's not cute anymore.

Trust me. There is *nothing* cute about a nude senior citizen.

I know what you're thinking, but you're wrong. Gump hasn't gone senile. The guy's still smart as a whip. He's just gone bananas.

It happened about a month ago. Mom's cell rang right in the middle of dinner. No one's allowed to even *touch* their phones during meals, but Mom could see it was Donna, so she took it.

Donna is Gump's fourth wife. The first one was Sandra. She was Mom's mother. She died before I was born. Then there was Nikki, who Mom calls Quickie, because she only lasted a few months. Then there was Misty, who Mom calls Mistake, because I guess she was.

And then there's Donna. Mom calls her The Saint, and she's not even joking. We all love Donna. Gump's not the easiest guy to get along with, but Donna always managed to do it. At least, until right then, that is.

Mom put down her fork and picked up her phone. All I could hear was Donna wailing away. My mouth was full of mashed potatoes. I gulped them down in one big blob and stared at Mom. My heart was going crazy. I thought Gump must have died. I could tell by the way Mom was clutching her shirt that she did too.

I was supposed to see Gump the weekend before, but I'd canceled because I wanted to hang out with my friends. I looked at Mom with her phone in her hand and her face gone white. I had the horrible feeling I'd never see him again.

"Donna," Mom said. "Take a breath, honey. I can't understand you." She looked across the table at Dad, who was smiling the way parents do when their kid is spurting blood all over the place and they're trying to act like everything is going to be fine.

Donna said something. I couldn't make out the words. All I could hear was the squeak of her voice.

Mom went, "Gump did *what*?"

Donna said something else.

Mom went, "Seriously?...Why?"

More squeaking from Donna.

Then Mom cracked up. She had her hand over her mouth so Donna wouldn't hear, but we all knew that look. Gump had done something ridiculous. In other words, the usual.

Phew, I thought.

I mean, like GIANT *phew*. I'd never been so relieved to hear that Gump was causing trouble again. I chuckled, shook my head and went back to eating my dinner. I'd call him when I had the chance.

Mom was doing her best to sound concerned, but it wasn't working. She had to do a lot of fake coughing to cover up her laughing. "Oh, you poor thing! Really?...That old goat. I don't know how you've put up with him as long as you have. But don't worry. The cops will pick him up soon. Get them to drop him off at our place. We'll have a word with him. He'll come around."

There was a little more talk and a little more fake coughing, then Mom said, "Love you" and hung up.

She leaned back in her chair and wiped the tears off her face with the back of her hand.

"So?" Dad said.

"Gump and Donna had a fight about Wayne."

Lena went, "Big deal," and started picking the mushrooms out of her salad. I don't usually agree with Lena—she's my sister and a bit of a pain—but she was right this time. Gump and Donna fought about Wayne every day.

Dad said, "What did he pee on this time?"

Wayne was always peeing on something, and Donna was always going nuts about it. It was the only thing she couldn't handle.

Which reminds me. In case you haven't guessed, Wayne is a dog. A purebred Shih Tzu. If you don't know what a Shih Tzu looks like, just picture a fur ball with a squished face and a bow on top. Now imagine a lot of yapping coming out of the squished face. That's basically Wayne, only he's old too. He's blind and he smells and he snores even when he's wide awake, but Gump loves him. Donna does not.

"Oh, I don't know," Mom said. "Doesn't really matter what he peed on. Donna just finally had enough, and I don't blame her. She said, *Either that dog goes, or I do*. Gump didn't answer in time, so Donna told him she wanted a divorce."

Lena said, "Not another divorce!"

I thought the same thing. Gump nearly drove us crazy when he and Misty broke up. He went from cranky to cantankerous and stayed that way for months. Wayne was the only living thing that could stand to be around him until Donna came along.

"Donna didn't really mean it," Mom said and piled some more salad on her plate. "She just wanted to shock him into being reasonable for a change. But you know Gump. You poke him, and he'll just poke back harder. He said, *Fine. Don't bother getting yourself a fancy divorce lawyer. You want the shirt off my back? Well, take it! Take it all, in fact!* Then he stripped off his clothes right then and there and walked out the front door, completely naked."

Lena shuddered. "Eww. Gross!" She pushed her plate away.

Dad said, "Your father," and rolled his eyes. "This is a new low, even for him."

Mom grinned. "Yeah, well, bad relatives make good stories." She's a freelance journalist. Gump's always doing something she can turn into an award-winning article.

We were having chicken that night, and Dad had overcooked it. The skin was wrinkled and the meat had shrunk up so you could see the bare bones. I held up a drumstick.

"Is it just me," I said, "or does this chicken remind you a bit of Gump naked?"

Everyone laughed except Lena. She burst out crying and ran into her room. Mom glared at me (even though she'd been laughing too), then went to see if Lena was okay. Dad and I arranged the chicken pieces to look like Gump in various old-guy action poses. Dad insisted on using a little spinach from the salad to cover Gump's chicken privates.

Until about nine that night, Mom was more worried about Lena than Gump. (Lena has gotten all weird since she started high school. She's always running away from the dinner table crying about something.)

By ten Mom was beginning to wonder where Gump was. She called the police to report a missing person.

The cop asked her to describe what Gump was wearing. She didn't think it was funny when the cop laughed.

By eleven she'd organized all Gump's friends into a search patrol. She was just getting ready to meet them at the park when the phone rang.

My heart started pounding again. I was sure it was the hospital, calling with bad news. I was really starting to feel terrible about how long it had been since I'd visited my one and only grandfather.

Mom picked up the phone, listened for a second and then a smile burst out on her face. "Gump! Oh, thank goodness! Where are you?"

He said something. Her smile drooped. Then it disappeared. She said, "Don't be silly!" a few times and "I'll come and get you right away," but Gump clearly wasn't going for it. She argued with him for a while longer. Then she sighed and hung up.

"He's not coming home," she said, "and he's not putting his clothes back on either."

Dad put his arm around her and gave her a squeeze. "He can't keep up this nonsense for long, Angie. I mean, he's going to have to find someplace to eat and sleep soon. Where can he do that naked?"

"Funny you should ask," Mom said in a way that didn't sound funny at all. "I'll tell you where. Gentle Breezes Nudist Community for Active Seniors."

Dad's eyes got big, but he knew better than to laugh.

Until that very moment, I'd been pretty sure Gump was the only grown-up in the world who wanted to walk around naked. But I was wrong. Apparently, there are lots of people like that. They're called weirdos.

Sorry. I mean, nudists.

A bunch of them live in their own little butt-naked town about an hour from our place. It turns out that after his fight with Donna, Gump put Wayne in the car and drove straight there. Stark naked.

He's been there ever since.

It's driving my family crazy.

Donna misses him and worries he's going to catch some disease. She keeps saying, "It can't be healthy. All those naked people sitting on each other's couches." She wishes she'd never complained about a little dog pee.

Mom misses Gump too, but mostly she's mad at him. She's really busy these days with work and yoga and stuff like that. She doesn't have time for his "shenanigans." She also doesn't like how unhappy he's made Donna. (Donna cries so much these days, her face looks kind of like a pink cauliflower.)

Dad's upset because Mom is. "It's like walking on eggshells around here," he says. Mom can't get mad at Gump, so sometimes she gets mad at Dad instead.

Lena can't eat because she keeps picturing Gump naked. Mom says, "Oh, Lena. Don't be ridiculous. You've seen him in his bathing suit before and that didn't stop you. There's no difference." But we all know there is.

Everyone's done what they can to get Gump to come home. Mom's begged him. Dad had a man-to-man talk with him. Lena used her babysitting money to buy him a new golf outfit. (He sent it back without even a thank-you note.) Donna apologized. She even promised to put the couch in the garage and let Wayne pee on it whenever he wants, but Gump's stubborn. He claims he's perfectly happy to spend the rest of his life "in the buff." He absolutely refuses to get dressed.

Which wouldn't bother me that much except that now I have to go and spend a whole week with him.

Chapter Two

I'm in the car with my mother, speeding down the highway. She's acting like she hasn't noticed I'm still mad.

"Beautiful day," she says.

I pull my ballcap over my eyes and slump in my seat.

"Nice and warm," she says.

I ignore her.

"Did you bring sunscreen?"

I laugh so she knows just how dumb that question is. "I'm pretty sure Gump will have sunscreen," I say.

Mom goes, "Oh, right," and sort of chuckles. "He'd have a pretty nasty sunburn without it, wouldn't he?"

She flicks my cap off my eyes to see if I get her little joke.

I say, "It's not funny." I turn the radio way up and pull my cap back down.

"C'mon, Rupert," she says. "It's not going to be that bad."

"No. It's going to be worse! Lena feels sick just imagining Gump naked. I actually have to see him—*in the flesh*."

For some reason, my mother finds that funny.

"And not just Gump either. Everybody else is going to be naked too. Total strangers with their, like, *stuff* hanging out." I make a gagging sound.

I have absolutely no interest in seeing anyone nude, let alone a bunch of grandparents.

Mom pats my leg.

"Not everybody's going to be naked, Rupe. I called the lady in charge of Gump's townhouse complex. She was very nice and sounded perfectly normal. She explained that nudism is a lifestyle choice. There's nothing icky about it. It's just about people wanting to feel more at home in their bodies. And anyway, she specifically said that Gentle Breezes was 'clothing-optional' and 'family-friendly'. Lots of grandchildren come to visit. Some of the residents will probably even have clothes on."

"A normal parent wouldn't make their kid go somewhere where only *some* of the people have clothes on. You know that, don't you?"

"Oh, you," she says and gives one of those little *tra-la-la* laughs.

"If it's so nice and non-icky, why don't *you* go then? Sounds like it would be just your thing. You're the get-in-touch-with-your-inner-whatever person around here. Not me."

Mom hums along to the song on the radio. She apparently enjoys ruining my life.

"Seriously. How come?" I keep at her. "No, don't tell me. I know. Because you've got some big assignment for the magazine. And Dad can't go because he's so bogged down at work. And— funny—but Lena's really busy too! She barely has enough time to text her friends a thousand times a day. You can hardly expect her to visit her actual *grandfather*."

Mom shakes her head like I'm being ridiculous.

"The truth is that none of you guys want to do it either," I say. "I'm just the sucker who got stuck with it."

"Rupe. It's not that and you know it. We've been through this. Gump was so thrilled last fall when we arranged for you two to go deep-sea fishing this summer. And I know the situation has changed a bit since then, what with the nudism and all. And I agree a week at Gentle Breezes isn't quite the same as a week on the ocean, but it's not really about *where* you go, is it? It's about spending time together, just the two of you."

"*Spending* time? More like wasting time. I didn't even want to go *fishing* with him! I'm thirteen. I'm too old to hang out with my grandfather—even if he has his clothes on. Frankly, I've got better things to do."

Mom drops her jaw like that's such an appalling thing to say, but it's true. I can think of lots of things I'd rather be doing. And I'm not even talking about going to the skateboard park or working on my parkour moves or sitting in front of the TV all day eating nachos. Pretty much anything other than unclogging a plugged toilet would be better than staying six days at a nudist colony with Gump.

I'm just about to tell Mom exactly that when traffic on the highway suddenly slows to a stop.

"I wonder what's happening." Mom opens her window and sticks her head out. "Looks like nothing's moving for miles."

She checks the time on the dashboard, then closes her eyes. "Argh. Gump's going to have a fit." Gump expects people to be on time, and Mom never is.

I grit my teeth. Somehow the thought of Gump having a tantrum naked is so much worse than him freaking out fully clothed.

The traffic crawls along until we see what the problem is. There's a police roadblock. A cop is stopping every car.

When it's finally our turn, Mom rolls down her window and smiles in this totally fake way. "Is there a problem, officer?" she says.

He's a big guy with mirrored sunglasses and veiny hands. He leans one arm on the roof of the car. "Not yet." He smiles. "But that's why we're stopping people. Where you headed?"

Mom says, "Gentle Breezes."

The cop raises his eyebrow like, *wow.* I bet he didn't take us for a couple of nudists.

"Okay, well, I'd advise you not to go out in the woods while there. A panther's just been spotted in the area."

Mom and I both go, "A panther?!"

The cop nods. "That's what I said too, but you heard right. It's definitely a panther. Young male, by the looks of it. Someone got a picture of him on their cell phone."

"What would a panther be doing way up here?" I say. "They're from South America." (I'm a big *Planet Earth* fan.)

"Yup. That's where they should probably stay too, but you know people these days. Everybody wants an exotic pet. Or think they do until they get it home and realize they can't take care of it. I've seen tigers and pythons and baby black rhinos just dumped on the side of the road because they got too big for the rec room." He shakes his head.

I want to ask him some more questions, but he taps the hood of our car and waves us on. "If you see the panther, call 9-1-1—but don't go near him. He's probably hungry. And when those big cats get hungry, they get dangerous."

We head off.

"Finally, some good news!" I say.

Mom gives me the side-eye. "How's a hungry panther good news?"

"There's hope it'll maul me before I have to visit Gump."

"Don't even say that, Rupe! I mean it." Mom slows way down so she can glare at me. A car behind us honks and zooms past.

"Okay, okay," I say. "Keep your eyes on the road. I was only joking...sort of."

Mom doesn't laugh. She just hunches over the wheel and stares at the road.

"Look. I know you're not happy about visiting Gump," she says after a while. "But I need you to go. I'm worried about him. I don't think there's anything wrong with nudism. I just think there's something wrong with it for *him*. He's not doing it to be closer to nature. He's doing it to be farther away from us. He's isolating himself. And no matter what I say to him or your dad says to him or even Donna, he won't listen. He's cutting himself off from the people who love him, and he's an old man. He needs us."

Mom's eyes have gotten all shiny. "I think you're the only one who can change his mind."

"Me? How? I can't argue with him about this. You know what he's like. He'd eat me up. I'd have a better chance with the panther."

"You don't have to argue with him. Just being there will make the difference. I know you haven't seen a lot of him recently, but you two were always so close. Seeing you again will make him realize how much he's missing. He's not stupid. It's going to dawn on him that he can't go bowling with you naked or take you out for pizza naked. He'll figure out pretty fast how much he's losing out on. Then he'll climb back into his clothes and come home."

I seriously doubt that, but I don't say so.

We drive along without talking. There's a new Justin Bieber song playing on the radio. My mother somehow knows all the words to it. I didn't like it before, but now I really hate it. When the song ends, the weather guy comes on and warns about a heat spell later in the week.

Mom says, "Sounds like you might be glad that you don't have to wear clothing either."

I go, "Ha-ha," but not as nastily as I could have. I can tell she's upset. Other than us, Gump's all Mom has. She was an only child. Her mother died when she was young. Her cousins all live in Australia.

She wipes the corner of her eyes like she has allergies or something, but I know she's just trying not to cry.

That makes two of us. The thought of spending a week with my nudist, weirdo grandfather makes me feel like crying too, but I can't think of any way out of it. Not that I didn't try. When Mom first talked about me going to Gentle Breezes, I'd thought she was joking. When I realized she was serious, I got my friend Noah to write a fake email inviting me to a fake camp that's free of fake charge for this week only. Mom almost fell for it until she noticed that it came from Noah's mother's email address.

Then I decided to break a bone. I figured Mom's not cruel enough to send me away wounded. I got a big rock and dropped it on my bare foot. It really hurt—and it didn't even break anything. I gave up on that idea.

I also tried my best to get a fever, a rash and a nasty cold, but Mom was onto me. She found the heating pad I'd put on my forehead. She spit on her finger and rubbed the red ink dots off my skin. Then she said if I didn't want to sneeze, I should stop putting pepper up my nose.

I'm desperate! I said.

You're going, she said. She's as stubborn as Gump.

We've been driving for almost an hour when Mom pipes up, "We're just about there!" As if that's a good thing. I look up and see the first sign for Gentle Breezes.

All I can think is, I should have dropped a bigger boulder on my foot when I had the chance.

Chapter Three

Gentle Breezes is a gated retirement community with a security guard at the entrance to keep the bad guys out. (Lots of old people live in gated communities. They worry about being safe. Can you imagine how much scarier it must be for old *naked* people?)

The guard is nice and—yay!—fully dressed. He slides open the window of his little shed and asks us who we're visiting.

Mom says, "Alan J. Smithers."

The guard laughs. "Head right in," he says. "Gump's waiting for you in the village square. Just keep following the road. You can't miss it."

We drive down a long road winding through the woods. After about ten minutes we come to a stop sign. Right in front of it is what I'd normally call civilization. There are lots of beige buildings with shops and offices and sidewalks and trees and bike racks and planters full of flowers. Everything is neat and tidy and ordinary. It's kind of like a little town you'd see on a television commercial. Only it's not. It's a nudist colony.

Mom pulls over and parks on the main street in front of an ice-cream parlor. There's a big picture in the window of a giant chocolate sundae.

It seems weird to me. Do naked people ever get hot enough for ice cream? I don't even want to think about it.

We get out of the car. I hear a cranky voice in the distance go, "Angie! Over here!" I look up and there's Gump sitting on a bench in the little town square. The bench is right next to a statue of a naked guy with a long beard and seriously ripped abs. Gump and the statue look like a really amazing before-and-after picture, with Gump definitely the before part.

Gump's wearing flip-flops and a fishing hat. Wayne is sitting on his lap, so I can't tell if he's wearing anything else. Luckily, Gump doesn't get up when he sees us.

Mom and I cross the street. We have to jump out of the way when a bicycle speeds by. The woman riding it calls out, "Sorry! Didn't see you!" and keeps pedaling past. She's a large lady and she's not young, and she's totally naked except for a red helmet that says *Speed Demon!* on the back.

"Wow. Look at her go!" Mom says.

"No, thank you," I say. I'm not going to look at anything I don't have to.

"Trying to get yourselves killed?" Gump says when we get to the bench.

The thought appeals to me—especially when I realize that, yes, my seventy-five-year old grandfather is indeed out in public, in broad daylight, without any clothes on. (If you can't picture what that looks like, imagine a Mexican Hairless cat, only human and with a hat on.)

"How are you doing, Dad?" Mom says. She only calls him Dad when she's upset with him. She bends over and gives him a super-awkward hug. (Hugs with Gump are awkward at the best of times.)

"I'd have been better if you hadn't kept me waiting in the hot sun all day.

I thought you said you were going to be here at one."

"It's only ten after, Dad. We got held up because there was a police roadblock. Believe it or not, someone just spotted an escaped panther in the woods and the police—"

"A panther?!" He snorts out a laugh. "You think I've gone soft in the head or something, Angela?" He only calls her Angela when he's upset with her. "A panther. Some excuse that is! You just don't want to be here. Well, fine by me! Who cares? I got all the new friends I could want." He raises his hand and waves at an old man jogging by. "Looking good, Ron!"

The guy seems a little surprised but waves anyway. "Thanks," he calls back, "but it's Bill!" He keeps going.

Gump shrugs and goes, "Ron, Bill—I always get those two guys mixed up."

I laugh a little because I don't believe him.

Gump turns and looks me up and down. "Aren't you hot? Peel off a few layers before you faint. This is a nudist colony, not the blinking Antarctic. You stick out like a sore thumb, wearing that crazy parka thing."

"It's a hoodie, Gump," I say, "and it's not crazy. Everybody wears them."

"Not around here they don't! We're all in the buff, and you should be too. You know what they say. When in Rome, do as the Romans do."

I bug my eyes out at Mom.

She raises her hand like *don't worry,* then turns to Gump. "Dad. I talked to you about this. Rupe is more comfortable as he is."

Gump makes one of those *pah* sounds pop bottles do when they get shaken up before opening. "Kids today. So uptight."

He stands up and starts walking away. There's no Shih Tzu to block the view from behind. His bum looks sort of sad and deflated. It reminds me of a couple of balloons the week after a birthday party. I slam my eyes shut and try to erase what I just saw.

Mom says, "Where are you going, Dad?"

"Back to my townhouse to feed Wayne. Poor little pup practically starved to death waiting for you two. Guess you don't care about *him* either."

"Do you need any help?" Mom starts following him. Gump swings around.

"No, I do *not* need any help! You think I can't look after my own doggone dog? I don't need any help from anyone. So why don't you just skedaddle—and take Mr. Hoodie-Head with you too, while you're at it!"

"Dad! You don't mean that. Now be reasonable. I'll come and help you make lunch, then Rupe will—"

"No, I said! You want to know who needs help? That silly Donna. Talking to me like I've lost my marbles! She's the one with the problem. Now get going!"

He gives a little flick of a wave goodbye, turns around and keeps walking.

Mom stops in her tracks and shakes her head. After a while she puts her arm around my shoulder.

"You know what, Rupe?" she says. "I think you should come home after all. I was hoping Gump would have softened up by now, but he's worse than ever. So c'mon. How about we stop for a burger on the way home?"

Yay, I think. Good old Gump! He finally came through when I needed him. "Okay," I say, "but only if I can get my burger...*all dressed*."

"Good one," she says, and we bump fists. We head back to the car.

I text Noah. **I'm free!!!!!! Meet me @ skatepark @3**

I put my phone in my pocket. I'm just about to get into the passenger seat when I turn and take one last look back. I catch Gump checking over his shoulder to see where I am.

I only see his face for a second, but I know exactly what he's thinking.

He's thinking I'm following him.

He's *hoping* I'm following him.

I sigh and close the car door. "I'm going to stay after all, Mom."

"Really?!" I can tell she's wondering now if that's a good idea. "You're sure?"

I nod.

She musses up my hair and gives me a hug. "You're a good kid, Rupe." She says goodbye and gets in the car.

I text Noah again. **NVM**

And then I run after Gump.

Chapter Four

Of course I'm going to stay. What choice do I have? If I leave, both Mom and Gump will be sad. If I stay, there's a tiny chance Mom will turn out to be right, and I'll be able to convince Gump to come home where he belongs.

I holler, "Gump! Wait up!" I know he hears me. I see him jump. But he keeps walking past the drugstore and the deli and the people sitting out under big umbrellas at the sidewalk café. (If they're so worried about getting too much sun, why don't they put some clothes on?)

I watch for a while, and then I sigh and run after him. It's too hot for a hoodie, but I'm not going to give him the satisfaction of taking it off.

He's almost made it to the sports field at the end of the main street by the time I catch up. I reach out and put my hand on his shoulder. "Gump! Stop. C'mon."

He turns and looks at my hand like it's a dead fish. He brushes it off and keeps walking. "I thought you were going home with your mother," he says.

"I changed my mind."

"Oh yeah? Why's that?"

We walk by four old ladies playing a very active game of nude tennis. It makes me wonder the same thing.

"I said I'd stay, so I'm staying."

"Yeah, well. Don't do me any favors, pal."

"I'm not." I'm doing Mom a favor. (I didn't say that.)

Wayne starts yapping, and Gump starts baby-talking to him about the mean boy who made him miss his lunch. (He calls it "wunch.") Then he turns to me, all Mr. Crabby again, and says, "Well, you're going to have to look after yourself. Your parents can't be saddling me with some kid all week and expect me to play babysitter. When I was your age, I was looking after myself. Used to spend two weeks every summer in the woods, hunting and fishing. Nobody was signing me up for after-school banjo lessons or buying me fancy headies, that's for sure."

"It's a hoodie. And I bought it myself."

"Just as bad! Waste of good money. What do you need clothes for?"

I let that go. I know Gump. He's just trying to pick a fight.

We turn the corner and walk along the other side of the sports field. I have to keep finding new things to look at. Everybody insists on being outside and doing things nude people shouldn't be doing. People are gardening and slacklining and having outdoor yoga classes. Every so often someone wanders up to us stark naked and wants to pat Wayne. Gump's as sweet as pie with them, but I'm not fooled. He's no happier to see them than he was to see me. He's just acting nice to bug me.

We finally get to Gump's place. He's in the very last townhouse on the street, right at the edge of the woods. When I complain about how long it takes to get there, he says, "I like my privacy."

Butt naked, but he likes his privacy.
Right.

He takes the key hanging off Wayne's
collar and opens the door. (I kind of
wondered where nudists keep their keys.
Who knows what they do with their
cell phones.) The townhouse isn't ugly
or anything, but it's pretty bare. The
main room only has a couch, a couple
of chairs and a big flat-screen TV on the
wall. It sure doesn't feel very homey, not
the way Donna's place does. It makes me
kind of sad.

"Here." Gump hands me Wayne.
"Watch him while I make his lunch.
If he looks like he needs to go wee-
wee, take him outside. I don't own this
furniture."

Gump heads into the kitchen.
I go straight outside. (As far as I'm
concerned, Wayne *always* looks like
he's going to pee.) I take the back door
because I figure I won't run into any

nudists in the little yard behind Gump's house.

I figured wrong. I've just put Wayne down when I look up and there's a lady standing on the other side of the fence. She's wearing big dangly earrings and reading glasses on a cord around her neck and, I'm pretty sure, nothing else. Luckily, the fence covers the worst of it.

"You must be Gump's grandson! I'm Brenda. I live next door. I'd come around and give you a hug, but I know how teenage boys hate to be hugged!" She puts her hand over the fence, and we shake. "My grandson won't let me near him! Anyway, I heard you were visiting and wanted to see if you and Gump would like to drop by for dinner tonight."

The answer, of course, is no. There's no way I can have dinner with a bare-naked lady. It's bad enough talking to her outside, where I at least have trees and clouds and grass to pretend to be fascinated with.

"Sorry," I say. "We can't. We have plans."

"Well, how about lunch tomorrow then?"

"Um…we're probably going to be gone for a couple of days."

"Oh, well, I'm sure we'll be able to find *something* that works for all of us. I have to run off to my Zumba class now, but let me check my daytimer and get back to you. I'd hate to have you here for a whole week and not have the chance to get you over for a meal!"

She jiggles off into her townhouse next door. I dart back into Gump's place before anyone else can pop by to say hello. I decide I'm going to hide inside with the doors locked for the rest of the week. I hope Gump has Netflix.

Gump's at the stove, cooking. He turns around when he hears me come in.

He's wearing an apron. It has *I'm with Stupid* printed on it, followed by an arrow that just happens to be pointing my way.

"What could you possibly be worried about getting a stain on?" I say. "You aren't wearing any clothes."

"I'm not worried about stains!" He rolls his eyes. "I'm worried about getting burned. Only a fool would cook bacon naked."

I consider saying *Obviously* but decide against it. Hearing the word *bacon* makes me realize I'm hungry. I haven't eaten since breakfast, and it's almost two o'clock now. I grab a nice crispy piece from the pan. The fat jumps up and sizzles on my hand. I see what he means about the apron.

Gump grabs the bacon back and throws it into a dog dish.

"That's for Wayne. Cook your own." He turns off the stove and looks around. "And by the way, where is he?"

"Who?" I say, not really caring. Gump was a cook in the navy, and he's really good at it. I'm kind of annoyed he's making food for some yappy little fleabag and not for me.

"Who do you think? Wayne!"

"He's just in the backyard." I retrieve the bacon from the dog dish. When I'm hungry, I have no pride.

Gump's face goes beet red. "Rupe!"

I'm like, "Chill. I'll make more." I can't believe how he's freaking out over one measly strip of bacon. Then he goes, "You can't leave Wayne alone out there! He's blind!"

Oops. I hadn't thought of that.

Gump runs out into the backyard, screaming, "Wayne! Waynie!" He's practically crying.

I drop the bacon back into the dog dish and go outside. Gump's in full disaster mode. His head's flipping from side to side like he's watching a super-fast game of Ping-Pong.

I look around the little backyard. The lawn's about the size of your average rec room. On one side there's the fence, dividing Gump's yard from Brenda's. On all the other sides, it's just woods.

It doesn't take long to see that Wayne's not in the yard.

"Where was he when you saw him last?" Gump says.

"I dunno. Just, like, here, I guess. I was talking to Brenda and…" I realize I was so busy trying not to look at Brenda that I wasn't watching Wayne. He could have trotted off before I even went back inside.

I don't like the look on Gump's face. I can handle him being mad—I'm used to that—but he looks terrified.

"He couldn't have gone far," I say, although I don't know that for sure.

I've never even seen Wayne walk. Gump always carries him.

"Yes, he could! When Wayne gets disoriented, he panics. And when he panics, he scampers. He could be anywhere!"

I notice a small trail of doggie do just at the edge of the yard.

"Looks like he went this way," I say, thinking that will make Gump feel better. But it doesn't.

"The woods! He's in the woods!" he gasps, and then, before I can stop him, Gump's in the woods too.

Chapter Five

I follow him into the forest. Apparently, Gump scampers when he panics too. I'm almost having trouble keeping up with him. The forest is cool and green and jam-packed with trees. I've never seen so many trees.

I know that sounds like a real city-kid thing to say, but hey. I'm a city kid. Closest I get to a forest is the park near our house where Gump and I used to fish. The woods there are all neat and tidy, like someone comes in every so often and vacuums up the dead leaves and branches.

Nobody does that here. The ground is covered with rocks and roots and other stuff to trip over, but it isn't slowing Gump down. He's leaping over things and under things like he's in some sort of seniors' nude track-and-field event. The whole time, he's screaming for Wayne. It would be funny if it wasn't so sad.

He scrambles up a hill. He doesn't seem to care that his bum's in my face or that he's covering me with the dirt and pinecones he's kicking up. I stop to cough some of it out. Gump darts around a big boulder and out of my sight.

Then suddenly the screaming stops.

I race to catch up with him. I find him leaning against a tree, panting. He has one hand on his chest. His face is red and all scrunched up like he's trying really hard to remember something.

Now *I'm* terrified. I know he won't admit it, but I can see he's in pain. Gump had a little heart attack last year. Donna made him change his diet and even got him to do some relaxation exercises. According to Mom, he's been fine ever since, but still. It's scary seeing him with his face like that.

I touch his arm. "Gump. Are you okay?"

He swats my hand away, and his eyes pop open.

"I would be if you hadn't gone and lost my dog!" He starts scampering again, but not as fast as before. He's not screaming anymore either. I don't think he has the breath.

Maybe it's because he's finally quiet, but I can hear something now.

A yap.

An irritating yap.

Gump's ears aren't so good anymore, so I don't think he hears it. I go, "Wayne! Wayne!" The yap gets louder. Even Gump can't miss it now. He stops and cups his hand behind his ear. He gets this big smile on his face, then starts running toward the noise.

"We're coming, Waynie boy! Stay put, little buddy! We're almost there!"

We take a few wrong turns and, once, almost fall off a mini cliff, but we manage to find Wayne pretty fast. He's tucked behind a rock. He must have tumbled into a little gully and couldn't get himself out.

When he realizes Gump has come to the rescue, Wayne goes nuts. He's like some wind-up toy. He's wagging everything he's got to wag. Gump picks him up, and the two of them yap and whine and lick each other's faces for ages. It's kind of touching, in a disgusting sort of way.

I sit on a rock and watch. I don't hurry them. I want Gump to catch his breath. He looks so weak and small, sitting there in just an apron.

Maybe that's why I suddenly think of that picture Mom has of us on the fridge. I'm just a little bare-naked baby in it. Gump still had some hair back then and some meat on his bones too. We're at the beach. Gump's holding me up high while a wave crashes over him from behind. He gets soaked but somehow manages to keep me dry. I've got this expression on my face like, *What the heck just happened?* Gump's laughing.

I realize I'm the one who's looking after him now.

"C'mon. Let's get going," he says and stands up.

"Relax," I say. "No need to hurry."

"Is so." He starts walking away. "This little fella's starving."

I forgot Wayne hasn't eaten. I'm pretty sure he and Gump will keep complaining until he's fed, so I say, "Okay." I get up and slap the tree dandruff off my jeans. "But if we're trying to get to your place, we should be heading the other way."

Gump rolls his eyes. "What are you talking about? The townhouse is due east!" Then he leans into Wayne's ear and goes, "Can you believe this guy? Some downtown clown trying to tell an old trailblazer like me how to find my way home. Pah!"

He scampers off in the wrong direction.

Or, at least, I think it's the wrong direction. I look around. I'm not so sure anymore. That's the weird thing about trees. They all look the same.

I follow Gump. I just want to get out of here as fast as possible. Now that we've found Wayne, I remember that he's not the only hungry animal prowling the woods. There's a panther we've got to worry about too.

We walk a good twenty minutes with no sign of Gentle Breezes. No sign of anything, in fact, except trees and rocks and more trees.

"See?" I say. "We went the wrong way. We should be there by now."

There's only one thing Gump hates more than admitting he's wrong. That's admitting someone else is right. No way is he going to follow my suggestion. He sets off in another direction entirely.

"Are you *sure* this is the right way?" I say. This direction seems the wrongest one yet.

He stops. Turns around. Points up through the trees. "Look at the position of the sun," he says. "What does that tell you about where we are right now?"

I squint up at it. "Not a thing," I say.

"My point exactly. You don't have a *clue* how to get us out of here! I, on the other hand, used to spend two weeks every summer in the wilderness—by myself. I know what I'm doing. So why don't you quit slowing us down with your dang fool comments." He turns around and starts walking again. "I wouldn't like to leave a defenseless creature alone in the woods, but I will if I have to."

I growl silently, then head off after him. It's sort of to keep an eye on him but mostly because I don't know what else to do. I try to believe he might actually know what he's doing.

An hour later we stop again.

"What now?" I sound cranky, but I'm really just worried.

"Whaddya think?" he says.

"Your heart's not acting up again, is it?"

"Not mine!" He points at Wayne as if he doesn't want him to know we're talking about him. "Someone else has a bad ticker too—and all this tromping through the backwoods isn't helping it any." Gump looks at me like we all know whose fault *that* is.

"Well, we must be almost there," I say. "We've been walking for ages."

Gump says, "Yeah," but he looks away when he says it. That's when I realize he has absolutely no idea where we are. He might have been an expert trailblazer when he was a kid, but that was a long, long time ago.

I'm lost in the woods with a blind Shih Tzu, a naked geezer and—somewhere out there—a hungry panther.

I have no idea how we're going to get out of this mess—until suddenly I have one of those *duh* moments.

I say, "Why don't I check where Gentle Breezes is on Google Maps, just to see how far we've got to go?" I reach into my pocket for my phone.

But my pocket's empty.

Chapter Six

My phone must have fallen out of my pocket while we were scrambling through the woods looking for Wayne. Gump and I search for it for ages, but it's no use. There are leaves and branches everywhere, and we're not even sure which way we came from. Plus, to make matters worse, the sun's going down.

Mom's going to kill me. It was a brand-new phone.

"No use looking for it in the dark," Gump says. "I suggest we bunk down for the night."

"What? Here?" I look around. There's nowhere to sleep here.

"Got any other suggestions?"

I don't.

I sigh and lie down on the flattest piece of earth I can find. It's hard, and there's a pointy rock sticking out that gets me right in the spine. I move, but there's another one that gets me in the hip. I sit up and pat the ground. There's a root or a rock or something wet and squishy wherever I put my hand. I decide to stick with the first place. I lie back down and close my eyes. I try not to think about the panther.

"What in tarnation are you doing?" Gump is standing right over me, glaring down. Once again I thank my lucky stars for that apron. "You're not just going to lie on the ground, are you?"

I sit up. "You're the one who said this is where we're sleeping."

"You never slept in the woods before, Buster?"

"No. What do you think I am? A raccoon or something? Why would I sleep in the woods when I've got a bed?"

He gives one of those "kids today" eye rolls. "Who says you can't have both? Get up and I'll show you."

He shakes his head and walks away. His bum is so white it almost glows in the dark. No wonder they call it a full moon.

He bends over and starts filling his apron with leaves. Then he stomps around on the ground like he's trying to find a place strong enough to hold all 103 pounds of him. When he finds a spot he likes, he dumps the leaves there.

"C'mon," he says. "You want a comfortable place to sleep? Well, better get to work then."

I gather up an armful of leaves. Most of them end up falling back on the ground before I have a chance to dump them on the pile. After a couple of armloads, I get a brilliant idea. I take off my hoodie and tie it backward around my waist. Now I've got an apron too. I might look like Little Bo Peep, but it works. I fill it up and unload it onto my so-called bed. Easy peasy.

Gump doesn't stop except to give Wayne a pat or to complain about my choice of leaves. "You want to sleep on wet leaves? Fine by me. That's your side of the bed then."

"Maybe if you had some clothes on, the wetness wouldn't bother you so much."

"Yeah, well, maybe if you'd looked after Wayne like you were supposed to, we wouldn't be here in the first place."

I sigh and go to get more leaves. Only the ones on the very top are dry enough for Old Mr. Picky-Picky. I find a nice stash behind a boulder and bring them back.

"You expecting to sleep on a king-size mattress or something?" Gump shakes his head. "We don't need any more leaves! We need some blankets."

"Yeah, well, good luck with that."

"I don't need good luck. I've got years of outdoor experience. Now give me a hand."

He starts stripping branches off fir trees. The smell reminds me of Christmas. I think of Mom and Dad and Lena. The house all warm and cozy. Everybody happy because there's lots of food and presents. And because we're all together too, I guess.

And then I remember the look on Mom's face the night that Gump went missing, and I realize how worried she must be about us.

"C'mon! Get to work! What are you stopping for? We need more branches than that." Gump is yanking away at a branch on some little tree. His arms are as skinny as a kid's. The muscles look like scrawny ropes moving back and forth. I find another tree and start tearing branches off too.

I tell myself not to worry. Mom will get a search party going for us.

Then I realize she won't even know we're in trouble. She said she'd call Thursday, and today's only Monday.

Then I realize *no one* will know we're missing, not even Gump's neighbors.

Am I ever sorry now that I told Brenda we'd be gone for a few days.

Me and my big mouth. How bad could eating dinner with a bare-naked lady be?

Nowhere near as bad as this.

"Okay." Gump drops an armload of branches onto the ground. "That should do it. Crawl onto the leaves and pull some boughs over you for cover. Trust me. You'll sleep better than you ever slept in your life."

I doubt that, but I do as I'm told. I can feel the cold from the earth coming through the leaves, but it's definitely better than before. I pull a bough over me and hope the panther won't be able to see me.

Gump crawls in on the other side. "And take your heady off and use it for a pillow."

"It's a hoodie," I say. "And I don't need a pillow."

I say it just to be snarky, but then I look over at Gump curled up beside me. His skin is covered in goose bumps.

"You're freezing." I pull off the hoodie and hand it to him. "Here. Take this."

He bats it away. "I don't need that crazy thing."

"You do so."

"Do not. I always sleep in the buff. Besides, I got Wayne to keep me warm."

Lot of good that will do. They're both shivering so hard now that the branches are shaking.

But there's no use fighting with Gump. I wait until I hear him snoring and then I drape my hoodie over him and Wayne.

I look up at the stars for a while. You can't see the stars in the city, and I like it that way. I find stars kind of creepy. They make me think of alien invasions.

I realize that's the last thing I have to worry about at the moment.

I roll over. Eventually I get too tired to be scared. I fall asleep.

Chapter Seven

I wake up because something is tickling my nose. For a second there, I think it must be Mom with a feather or a dirty sock or something. That's the type of thing she does. Why set an alarm when it's so much more fun waking your kids yourself? She's always coming up with diabolical new ways to do it.

Then something licks my nose.

Even Mom, I realize, wouldn't lick my nose.

I smell the pine needles and feel the lumpy ground. In a flash I remember I'm not at home. I'm in the woods.

With an escaped panther.

I jump up, screaming, "Run, Gump! Run!" I don't look back. I just burn out of there as fast as I can. I take about three steps and trip over the stupid branches. I land face first on the ground.

Something licks my nose again. I don't even need to open my eyes to know it's Wayne. I recognize his breath.

I realize it's been Wayne all along.

I groan and turn my head. Not that far away, I see Gump with an armful of branches. "Crikey," he says. "What was that all about? Trying to beat me to the bathroom or something?"

"Wayne licked my nose and scared me. I thought he was the panther."

"The panther!" Gump chuckles in a not-very-nice way. "That silly excuse of your mother's? Don't tell me you believe that nonsense, do you?

I sit up and rub my eyes. "Yeah. I do. The cop said—"

"Pah! There's no doggone panther around here. Now come and warm yourself up."

I look over and see Gump's got a campfire going. He and Wayne settle down beside it.

"Where'd you find matches around here?" I say.

"Who needs matches? All it takes is a couple of dry sticks and a little friction, and bingo! Raging fire."

"Why didn't we do that last night then? Would have been nice to have a warm bed." My whole body hurts. I stand up and stretch.

"Like you needed it. You slept like a baby." He throws a bough on the fire.

It sizzles, and smoke billows up. He pulls Wayne out of the way. "I knew I shouldn't have made the bed so comfortable for you. We lost half the day."

"What are you talking about?" I say. "It's barely morning."

"Barely morning?" He checks the sky. "It must be eight o'clock. Maybe ten after."

I raise my eyebrows. I don't believe him. "You can tell the time just by looking at the sun?"

"Can't you?"

It's too early to get into this with him, and my heart's still pounding after the panther scare. I sit down beside the fire. Wayne yaps, and Gump picks him up and moves him to the other side. "He doesn't like to be crowded. You know that."

I'm just about to roll my eyes when Gump says, "Breakfast?" He reaches into the pocket of his apron and dumps out a pile of blueberries. "Found a little patch not far from here," he says. "Good thing you finally woke up, because there weren't many, and Wayne and I were going to eat them all ourselves."

He hands them out like he's dealing cards. One for Wayne, one for him, one for me. Considering that Wayne only weighs about six pounds, I don't think he should get an even share, but I keep my mouth shut.

Some of the blueberries aren't quite ripe, and others are kind of squishy from being in Gump's pocket, but they taste delicious.

"So what's our plan?" I say once we're done "breakfast." I pull my hoodie out from under Wayne and put it on. Even with the fire, it's a little chilly this early in the woods.

"Don't know what yours is," Gump says, "but here's mine. I've had a chance to look around this morning. You threw me off my bearings yesterday, which is why we came in from that direction over there. Without you yammering at me today, I was able to get myself situated again. See that hemlock next to the boulder?"

He points at a droopy Christmas-tree-type tree.

"That's due east. We'll head that way, and unless you confuse me again, we should be back at Gentle Breezes by noon. I'll call your mother, and she'll have you home in front of your video games by two. That okay with you?"

"Perfect."

Gump finds a flat rock and uses it to dig up dirt to throw on the fire. As he's bending over to make sure it's out, I notice red marks all over his bum. (There are no secrets when your grandfather is a nudist.)

"Something bit you, Gump."

He reaches back and scratches. "Yeah. Well, that's the law of the jungle. Eat or be eaten."

"I bet you wish you were wearing clothes now."

"Well, you bet wrong, kiddo. Some of us are man enough to take it."

He throws more dirt over the fire and stirs it with a stick. When he's sure it's out, he picks up Wayne and starts walking toward the hemlock. I guess we're going. I follow him.

We've been slogging through the forest for quite a while when Gump says, "We're not far from water."

I'm really, really thirsty, so I hope he's right, but I don't have that much confidence in him anymore. Some trailblazer he turned out to be. I might be the reason we're in the woods, but I'm pretty sure he's the reason we're lost. "How do you know?" I say.

"Read the signs, Buster. Read the signs! Look how green everything's getting!" Now that he mentions it, I can see it's true. The leaves do look brighter. We keep walking, and pretty soon we come to a little pond.

The water's very still. It's covered in this scummy stuff, but I kneel down to scoop up some water anyway.

Gump goes nuts. "What's the matter with you, kid? Never drink still water! Or do you actually *want* to get the runs? Don't they teach you anything in school these days?"

"So what do I drink then? I haven't noticed any lemonade stands around here."

More head shaking from Gump. "You follow the water downhill! See the little brook that runs out of the pond? By the time the water flows over the rocks, it'll be clean. I don't know how you survive. Honest to Pete."

My mouth's so dry it seems mean to make me wait for a drink, but the last thing I want is diarrhea. (Wrong. Actually, the last thing I want is to be mauled by a panther. Close second is the runs.) I start doing that Wayne thing. I'm walking down the hill with my tongue hanging out. I'm even panting a little bit by the time we get to the bottom.

I'm wearing sneakers, but Gump's just in flip-flops. It can't be easy hiking through the woods in those, but he doesn't complain. He scrambles over the rocks and down the bank to the water.

The bank is muddy, but the water is clean and cool. I lie on my stomach and scoop handful after handful into my mouth. I've never been so thirsty in my life, and that includes the time I ate a family-size bucket of popcorn all by myself.

When I finally look up and see Gump, I scream.

Chapter Eight

Gump is completely covered in mud. Face, chest, legs, arms, little formerly white butt. He's standing there with one arm over his head, slapping mud into his armpit.

"Is this some kind of joke?" I say once I catch my breath.

"I don't joke," he says, which is, of course, a lie. "If you knew anything about wilderness survival, you'd know exactly why I'm doing this."

"Problem perspiration?" I say. Just a guess.

"No. But that's the thing with you city kids, isn't it? You all think there's something so terrible about the natural body."

"Yeah yeah. Enough with the nudist propaganda. What is it then?"

Gump scoops up another handful of mud and slathers it on the back of his neck. "A naked man, unprotected, will burn in the noonday sun in under an hour. Mud makes an excellent sunscreen."

"Not as good as clothes."

"Maybe, but clothes won't take the sting out of insect bites. Mud is very soothing." He reaches back and dabs some more mud on his bug-eaten butt. Even with their chocolaty coating I can see the welts. I almost feel sorry for him. The bugs didn't get me at all.

I take another swig of water just in case it's a while before we come across another stream. I wipe my face on my sleeve. "If you wore clothes, you wouldn't be covered in bites."

"And if you'd looked after Wayne, we wouldn't be stuck here having this conversation."

I climb up the bank. "Stuck? I thought you loved the Great Outdoors."

He pushes me aside and jostles past me with Wayne in his arms, who is yapping his little head off. "It *was* great until you came along. Now I'm not so sure."

We wander through the woods like that, bickering the whole way. It's funny. When I was little, I thought Gump knew everything. Now I just think he's a know-it-all. (Those two sentences sound the same, but they're totally different.)

It's also hard to take him seriously given the way he looks. It was bad enough when he was just skinny, naked and wearing that stupid apron. Now the mud he slapped all over himself has dried and is starting to crack. He looks like a very old lizard about to shed his skin.

It's starting to get warmer now too. I remember the guy on the radio saying we were in for a heat wave. Even in the woods, when the sun breaks through the trees it's almost hot.

I take off my hoodie and tie it around my waist.

"I'm hungry," I say.

"Yeah, well, join the club. You won't have anything to eat for a while." Gump reaches into his pocket and takes out a few blueberries. He feeds them to Wayne.

"Hey!" I say. "I thought you said there won't be anything to eat for a while."

"I said, *you* won't have anything to eat for a while. Only enough for Wayne."

"How come Wayne gets it?"

Gump stops and glares at me. His eyes look blue as a swimming pool next to the brown mud. "Why do you think?"

He turns and starts walking.

"No good reason," I say. "That's what I think."

"Oh yeah? Well, you're wrong." He keeps walking.

"Then why?"

"Because Wayne's the only person who cares about me."

I can't believe he's being so childish.

"Untrue." I race to catch up to him. "For starters, in case you didn't notice, Wayne's not a person."

"You're right. Sorry, Wayne. Didn't mean to insult you like that."

"And, secondly, lots of people care about you."

He doesn't even answer. He just goes, "Pah!" like it's a ridiculous idea.

"Donna cares about you," I say.

"Donna? Donna who? Oh, I know! You mean the lady who wants to divorce me."

"She wasn't serious. She just wants you to do something about Wayne's bladder problem."

Gump clamps a hand over Wayne's ears and goes, "Shh!"

"Okay, Mom cares about you."

"My daughter? The one who's too busy working to drop by occasionally?"

"She's got articles to write! You know that."

"Okay. Then how about my son-in-law and my granddaughter? What's their excuse?"

I'm all ready to launch into their excuses when I realize that's exactly what they are. Excuses. I even said so myself to Mom. I was the only person who didn't have a good enough excuse not to have to visit him.

Gump waves his hand at me before I can come up with something new. "Don't even bother!" he says. "I've heard it all before. No one can find time for me, but they all expect me to act the way they want me to act. Dress the way they like. Get the type of dog they approve of. Well, no, thank you very much. I don't need anyone."

Gump straightens his shoulders and tromps off like a little kid having a tantrum.

Something about this whole thing makes me feel sad. I realize Gump's not mad. He's hurt.

I catch up to him and go, "C'mon, Gump!" I wrap my arm around his shoulder. He tries to wiggle away from me, but I'm holding on tight. "You know we all…"

I was going to say *love you*, but instead I say, "Aaaaaaaaah!!!!!"

One moment we're both walking across a little clearing in the forest. The next moment, we're lying on top of each other at the bottom of a dark pit.

Chapter Nine

I feel a crunch when I land. It takes me a second to realize what it is. Or should I say *who* it is?

Gump groans, and I roll off him.

"Are you okay?"

He doesn't answer right away. He sits up slowly, rubbing his arm and wincing. He blinks to get used to the dark and looks around. Then he sucks in his breath as if something just stabbed him in the chest.

"What?" I say. "Is it your arm? Your heart? Can you walk? How many fingers am I holding up?"

"No!" He bats my hand away. "It's Wayne! Where's Wayne?"

The pit is mostly dark except for little bright spots where the sun breaks through the trees and shines down into the hole. I squint and pat the earth in the dark spots, but no luck.

"He's not here," I say. "But I'm sure he's okay. He's probably just—"

Gump loses it. He starts screaming, "Wayne! Waynie!" at the top of his voice.

When he finally takes a breath, I manage to hear a little pitter-patter of feet and some yapping.

"Relax, Gump. He's okay. See?"

We both look up, and there's Wayne peering over the edge of the pit. For a second I have a horrible feeling he's going to leap in too, but Gump raises one hand and goes, "Stay, boy! Stay!" And, believe it or not, Wayne does. (Wayne is not known for his obedience. He and Gump have a lot in common— although, thankfully, not the peeing on couches bit. At least, not yet.)

"Phew," I say. "That was close. Good thing he's okay."

"Okay?! What are you talking about? He's up there all by himself, blind and defenseless. Something could get him!"

"Like what? He's right *there*."

"What do you think? The panther!"

I go, "Pah!" just like Gump would if I'd said the same thing. "*You* were the one who said there's no panther."

"Yeah, well, now I'm not so sure. What if there is? That panther would gobble Wayne up like a peanut. A jelly bean. He'd be gone in a second. Heck, a good-sized squirrel could take Wayne down if it wanted to. Someone's got to save him!"

I don't like the way his face is going all red again. "Okay, okay. Just calm down, Gump. I'll get Wayne."

"How?" Gump begins to pace back and forth in the little pit. Two steps one way, two steps the other. "You're too short to get out of here. The walls are dirt. There's nothing to hold on to."

I'm thinking the same thing, but now's not the time to admit it. "I just need something to stand on, and then I can reach up and pull myself out."

"Brilliant," Gump says. "Wait there. I'll get the ladder."

I don't appreciate his sarcasm. "Gee, thanks, Gump. You're being very helpful."

And then it dawns on me. Maybe he *could* be helpful.

"Do you think you're strong enough to give me a leg up?" I say.

"What?! Of course I'm strong enough!"

He spreads his feet apart like a very skinny sumo wrestler, then clasps his hands together at his waist and goes, "What are you waiting for?"

I put my left foot onto his hands and heave myself up.

Gump's hands give way immediately, and we both fall over.

As he's struggling to get up, I realize what the problem is.

"Gump," I say and help him to his feet.

"Yeah?"

"What's the matter with your arm?"

"Nothing. What are you talking about?" He waves his right arm in my face. "One hundred percent working order."

"Yeah, but what about this one?" I pick up his left arm at the elbow. It hangs loose, like he's a puppet with a broken string.

Gump pulls it back with his other hand and says, "It's just fallen asleep. It'll be fine in no time."

No, it won't, I think, but I don't say so. I've got to concentrate on finding another way out of here.

I scratch my head for a while, then notice a notch in the wall at about waist height. It's pretty small, but it'll do. I scrape away at it with my fingers until it's just big enough to squeeze my toes in. That'll give me a leg up.

"Okay, Gump," I say, "get your back under me and give my butt a push."

I barely have time to get my foot in the notch before Gump has practically catapulted me out of the pit. (He's getting back at me for suggesting he wasn't strong enough to help.) I grab a root to keep myself from falling back in. I flail my legs around until I manage to swing one up onto the ground, and then the other. (That's harder to do than it sounds, especially when there's a crazy old man screaming at you from one end and a stinky old dog licking your face at the other.)

"Any panthers?" Gump calls.

"No, we're good. Now I've just got to rescue you."

I crawl up onto my feet and look around for something I can use to pull Gump out with. I notice a lot of branches scattered on the ground. That's when I realize why we didn't see the pit in the first place. It's a trap of some type! A hidden hole to try and catch someone. Or something.

The panther maybe?

I don't even like to think about it.

I lie on my belly and lower a branch into the pit for Gump to grab on to. He tries, but he just doesn't have the strength in one arm to pull himself up. He falls back onto the ground and lets out a whimper. Wayne starts yapping and growling at me. I'm worried he's going to attack me for hurting Gump.

I get an idea. "Give me your apron," I say.

"Why?" Like I'm planning to steal it or something.

"You know the strap that goes around your neck?"

He looks at me like, *duh*.

"I'm going to get you to put your foot in it like a stirrup, so I can pull you up." He won't admit that's a brilliant idea, but he doesn't argue. He tosses me the apron. I lie on my belly. I hang on to the bottom of the apron and lower the top part down to him. "Okay. Step in and then hold on tight."

He does, and I heave as hard as I can. Good thing he's so skinny. It takes all my strength, but I manage to drag him up onto the ground.

We're both exhausted. We lie there for a few seconds to catch our breath, and then I get back to work. I help Gump back into his apron. (There's only so much I want to look at.) Then I untie my hoodie, take off my T-shirt and tear it in half to make him a sling.

Chapter Ten

After I wrap his arm in the sling and put my hoodie back on, I help Gump over to a comfortable spot by a tree. "You stay here," I say. "I'm going to find help."

"You? You couldn't find your way out of a paper bag! You stay. I'll go." Gump tries to stand, but his face scrunches up in pain.

"I'm going," I say.

"You're going to get lost," he says, but he leans back against the tree.

"No I'm not."

"How do you know?"

"I've got a plan." I take off one of my socks and start chewing on the edge.

He watches me, shaking his head. "And Donna complains about *Wayne*! Even *he* wouldn't chew on a cruddy old sock. How hungry are you anyway, Buster?"

"Not that hungry." I put my sneaker back on and pick at the hole in the sock until I find a thread. I pull it loose.

"What are you doing that for?" Gump hates not knowing what I'm up to.

I break off a bit of thread and tie it around a branch. "Markers," I say, "so I can find my way back." I go a little farther out of the clearing and tie another one.

Gump snorts. He has to admit it's a pretty smart idea, but of course he won't.

"If I don't find help, I'll find food," I say. "I'll be back soon."

I have no idea where I'm going or what I'm looking for, but ten minutes later I get lucky. I find some raspberries. I pick a bunch. They'll get squished if I keep them in my pocket, so I take off my other sock and put the berries there instead. Pretty soon my white sock is covered in big red blotches. I think how mad Mom's going to be about the stains.

Then I realize she won't be mad. She'll just be so happy to have me back.

I *have* to make sure Gump and I get back.

I need more than berries. I need help. I worry about Gump's arm. I worry about Gump having a heart attack while I'm gone. I worry the panther's going to get him.

I just plain worry.

I keep walking and tying markers on branches. I've almost used my whole sock. That's how far I've gone. After a while I think I hear something. Something sort of tinkly and far away. It's hard to hear over my crunching through the branches, so I stop.

Yes. I *do* hear something.

It's music. I go a little farther.

It's Justin Bieber. That song Mom likes. The one we heard on the radio.

For a second I think she must have come to find us. Then I realize that doesn't make any sense. She wouldn't be playing a Justin Bieber song. She'd be screaming for me the way Gump was screaming for Wayne.

What I hear is a radio. Someone is in the woods, listening to music.

I follow the sound, and pretty soon I see a path. The trees thin out a bit, and it's almost like I'm in a little farmer's field. There are rows of tall, dark-green plants. The leaves look familiar, but I can't think what they are. I tear a couple off and put them in my pocket. Gump will know. He and Donna love to garden.

I walk through the rows of plants. I start seeing signs that people have been here. There's an old rusty barbecue. A banged-up icebox painted in camo style. Some sleeping bags. And there's a lean-to shelter too. Someone built it against the side of a boulder and covered it with pine branches. It's sort of like what Gump did last night, except it looks kind of scary. What kind of person would be living way out in the woods like this?

I gulp. I want to go back to Gump, but what good would that do? An old, naked, wounded guy and a kid? How long would we survive in the woods alone? How long would we survive in the woods with a panther? I need help. I tell myself that whoever's here probably isn't that bad. I've just watched too many horror movies.

And anyway, it's broad daylight. Bad things don't happen in broad daylight.

I keep walking toward the sound of the music. And then I see someone. He's about a city block away. It's a guy. That's all I can tell. His back is to me, so I can't see what he looks like. He's tall, though, so he must be a grown-up. His hair is short, so he's not some crazy hillbilly guy who lives out in the woods, eating lost kids. He's holding something. A tool. I wonder if he's a lumberjack, here to cut down trees. Someone must have to cut down the trees so the plants can grow.

"Hey!" I call. He doesn't turn around. The radio must be pretty loud where he is. I run toward him and go, "Hey!" even louder. Now he turns around. He puts his hand over his eyes to block the sun so he can see me. I wave my arms over my head. He drops his hand. That's when I see he's not holding a saw or an ax or anything handy like that.

He's holding a gun.

A big gun.

And now he's running toward me.

I turn and boot it out of there. I just hope the guy doesn't notice the markers. I'm trying to follow them while jumping over rocks and around trees. I stumble and crack my knee hard against a root. I land on my sock full of raspberries, and red juice splats over me like blood. I get up and keep running, even though my leg is killing me. I don't have time to limp. I'm lucky I have a head start on the guy. Maybe I'll make it back to Gump before he catches up.

The guy's screaming at me to stop.

Ha. Like I'm stopping.

His voice seems to get softer, and for a while I think maybe I've lost him. But then it's loud again.

Finally I slide like a klutz into the clearing where Gump is still leaning calmly against the tree.

"What took you so long, Buster? I knew you wouldn't find any help. You shoulda just let me—"

"Shut up, Gump."

"Don't you tell me to—"

"Shut up. I mean it. We're in trouble."

Gump, unbelievably, shuts up.

"We've got to hide."

My first thought is the pit. But I look at Gump, barely able to move, and I realize we'd never get out. He's hurt worse than I thought he was.

I hear branches breaking and the guy swearing. He's getting close. I take Wayne, then grab Gump by his good arm and get him onto his feet. His face wrinkles in pain, but he doesn't make a sound. There's a big boulder not far from the tree. I drag Gump and Wayne behind it, pull some branches over top of us and hunch down beside them.

Seconds later the guy comes pounding into the clearing.

I'm terrified Wayne is going to start yapping. Luckily, I'm covered in raspberry juice. I put out my hand and let Wayne lick my fingers. That should keep him quiet for a while.

I can hear the guy panting as he catches his breath. He must be just on the other side of the boulder. Next thing I know, he's talking to someone.

"Looks like we've got an intruder," he says.

Silence for a beat. Then he says, "Yup, down by one of our pits." Another pause. "Don't think they fell in, but someone did. The branches have been moved."

He must be talking on a cell phone. "I'll keep looking. If we're lucky, he's fallen into one of the other ones. But don't worry. The crop's safe. I'll find him. I'll make sure of that. I'll follow the trail all the way to the bridge. That's the only way out."

He doesn't say anything more. I hold my breath. I let Wayne lick my arm right up to my elbow, until I'm sure the guy's gone. Then I poke my head out from behind the boulder.

"You can come out," I whisper and push the branches off.

I'm worried about Gump, but he's got a big smile on his face. "What do you think of Wayne's new lipstick?" he says. The white fur around the dog's snout is stained bright red from the raspberries.

"I can't believe you're laughing at a time like this," I say.

"What are you going to do?" Gump shrugs. "Gotta laugh!"

"Not when someone's trying to kill you! And I don't even know why he'd want to."

"You don't? It's obvious." Gump's trying to adjust Wayne's bow with his one good hand. "You stumbled upon the guy's crop."

"Oh, come on! What type of crop would people want to kill you for?"

"Ever heard of mari-ju-ana?" Gump says. And that's when I remember the leaves in my pocket. I pull them out.

He looks at them and sniffs. "That's it! You just found an illegal grow op, my friend. No wonder the guy's so mad. You rat on him and he'll end up in jail."

"What are we going to do?" I say.

"What else? Outsmart him."

Chapter Eleven

"He's got the gun, and I'm in flip-flops," Gump says, "so we can't outpower him or outrun him."

I figure Gump's flip-flops aren't the only reason we can't outrun him, but if ever there was a time to be positive, it's now.

"First thing we want to do is make sure he can't see us."

"Okay," I say. "How?"

"Natural camouflage. Remember that old war movie we watched? The one where the soldiers disguised themselves with branches?"

Of course I remember that movie! I loved how the soldiers looked like little moving bushes. I nod and immediately get to work. We gather up the boughs that used to cover the pit. I find the other half of my T-shirt on the ground. We rub it in dirt so it's not so white, then tear it into strips. We use the strips to tie the branches onto our heads and backs. Then I smear dirt all over my face, just to be on the safe side.

We look like really bad Christmas trees in the school holiday pageant, but it's the best we can do.

If we scrunched up on the ground, you might not know we were there. We even tie a few branches on Wayne. (He's not that keen on it.)

"Now what?" I say.

"We're going to follow him."

"What?!"

"Didn't you hear what he said on the phone? He's going down the path to the bridge. *The only way out of here.* If we find him, we'll find our way home."

"You think that's safe?" I say.

"No. But what's our choice? Dying here in the woods? No thank you. The hockey playoffs are on next week, and my team's got a decent chance of winning. Now help me up."

I've just got him on his feet again when we hear branches snapping and the sound of footsteps. We slip behind the boulder just as the guy shows up again.

He's talking on the phone. "I walked right to the bridge, but no sign of him... He's just a kid. I ain't too worried.

He'll never find his way out of here."
He laughs demonically.

I don't like this guy very much.

There's a pause and he goes,
"Whaddya mean, eaten by a panther?…
There's a panther in the woods? Quit
pulling my leg, Brady. You're just
saying that because you know I'm
scared of cats." He swears a few times,
and then he says he's heading back to
the camp.

I figure just a few more minutes
and we'll be in the clear. I have a pretty
good idea which direction he came
from, so we can probably find the path
home.

Then Wayne starts wiggling and
making little peeping noises. I shake my
head at Gump. I mouth, *Shut him up*,
but it's too late. Wayne begins to yap.

It's not his "I'm hungry" yap or his
"I need attention" yap. It's different.

I'm pretty sure it's his "I'm terrified" yap. I look up, expecting to see the guy pointing the gun at us, but that's not what's scaring Wayne.

It's the panther.

Chapter Twelve

The panther's back is up and its head is down, and it's slowly and silently moving across the clearing toward us. It's got big green eyes and long white teeth, and it's the scariest thing I've ever seen.

I figure we're dead meat. I know Gump and Wayne do too, because

Gump whispers, "Love you, Buster," and Wayne pees on me.

Then something weird happens. Wayne suddenly jerks his head the other way, and his ears perk up as if he senses something else.

I turn and look.

The guy is standing on top of the boulder with his gun pointed at us.

All I can think is, why's he pointing the gun at us and not the panther?

I just have time to realize he must have heard Wayne yap and come back into the clearing from the other direction.

He didn't see the panther. He has no idea it's skulking up behind him.

I'm just wondering if it would be a good idea to warn the guy when the panther pounces.

Not at us.

At him.

The guy doesn't know what hit him.

It's full-blown panic stations after that. I pull Gump onto his feet. He practically throws Wayne at me and goes, "Run! Run!" So I do.

I figure he's right behind me, but I'm wrong. I've just gotten to the edge of the clearing when I turn around to look.

I can't believe what I'm seeing. The guy is lying on the ground, screeching. The panther has his jaws clamped on his leg.

And there's Gump.

He isn't running. He's not trying to get away. He's standing between the open pit and the screeching man. What's worse, he's throwing stones at the panther.

I scream, "Gump! What's the matter with you? Stop! C'mon!"

The panther growls and looks back at the old naked guy covered in mud and branches. He must think Gump is crazy. I certainly do.

"Git, you numskull!" he screams at me over his shoulder. "Take Wayne and get out of here!" He hurls another stone. It flies over the guy and bounces off the panther's back.

"Please, Gump!" I'm begging him. "Quit bugging the panther. He's happy eating the other guy. C'mon!"

The guy starts screeching even louder at that.

"No," Gump says. "Can't leave a man like this." Then he picks up another stone—a big one this time—and beans the panther right in the head.

That did it. Now the panther's mad. He drops the guy's leg, growls and pounces at Gump.

He's so fast.

But, weirdly, Gump is even faster. He falls sideways. The panther pounces over him and lands right in the pit.

I run back to the clearing. My first thought is that Gump didn't fall on purpose. He had a heart attack.

I shake his arm. He doesn't move.

"Gump! Are you okay?"

I give him another shake. "Gump!"

I put my arms around him. He's so skinny and dirty and brave. I start to cry. I'm crying even worse than Donna did when Gump left her for Gentle Breezes, and I don't care how stupid I look.

Then I hear him groan.

I sit up. He rolls onto his side and starts spitting out dirt and pine needles.

He looks at me, eyes as bright as ever. "How I'd do?" he says.

The panther's growling in the pit, and the man's moaning on the ground.

"You did great," I say.

Chapter Thirteen

Gump won't let me hold the gun because I'm only thirteen, so he stands over the bad guy while I rifle through his pockets for his cell phone. I call 9-1-1 for help.

Then Gump tells me how to stop the bleeding, and I tie my hoodie around the guy's leg where the panther got him.

The whole time, the guy's going, "What just happened? What just happened?"

No matter how many times I try to explain, he doesn't believe me. He keeps asking if Gump is for real or if he's hallucinating.

I look at Gump, covered in branches and bruises and mud, standing there with a big stupid smile on his face. I tell the guy I'm not sure.

Epilogue

The bad guy went to jail. The panther went to the zoo. Gump got dressed and left Gentle Breezes, but not before Brenda had us all over for dinner at her house. (It was every bit as awkward as I thought it was going to be. On the plus side, she makes excellent burritos.)

Donna promised Gump she'd never divorce him. Gump promised her he'd buy diapers for Wayne.

I didn't promise Gump I'd see him more often, but only because I didn't need to. He knows I will.

Tonight I'm going over to his place to scream at the TV during the hockey playoffs. I can hardly wait.

Vicki Grant is the award-winning author of many novels for young readers, including *Hold the Pickles* and *Pigboy* for Orca Currents. Her novels have won a Red Maple Fiction Award, an Arthur Ellis Award and CBC's Young Canada Reads as well as been short-listed for an Edgar Award, CLA Children's Book of the Year and numerous Forest of Reading awards. Her books have been translated into more than twenty languages. She lives in Halifax, Nova Scotia. For more information, visit vickigrant.com.

For more information on all the books
in the Orca Currents series, please visit
orcabook.com.